CW00868796

Acknowledgements

My dearest son Dhiyan,
thank you for completing us.

Published by S&B 2016
Copyright Sunita Shah and James Ballance
ISBN 978-1-78808-654-7

The Jai Jais

Krishna

by Sunita Shah

Illustrated by James Ballance

Hello, my name is Krishna.

I am handsome,
playful and cheeky.

I was born in Mathura.

Mathura is near
the Yamuna river.

I was raised by
Nanda and Yashoda.

My brother is called Balrama.

I lived with the
cow herds in Gokul.

I looked after the cows.

There was a snake with many heads that hid in the River Yamuna.

It made people sad so I got
rid of the naughty snake!

I am very strong.

I fought the bad demon Kans.

I love butter.

I eat it from the pot.

My mum gets cross
and chases me.

People call me
the "Butter Thief".

I have a special friend
called Radha.

We like dancing together.

I can play the flute.

I love the sound of music.

I will always show you what
is right and what is wrong.

Glossary

Mathura
- city in the north central of India.

Gokul
- area of India south-west of the city of Mathura.

Demon Kans
- once the evil ruler of Mathura.